Book Club Edition

WALT DISNEY PRODUCTIONS

presents

The Christmas Helpers

Random House 🏠 **New York**

First American Edition. Copyright © 1984, 1985 by Walt Disney Productions. All rights reserved under International and Pan-American Copyright Conventions. Published in the United States by Random House, Inc., New York, and simultaneously in Canada by Random House of Canada Limited, Toronto. Originally published in Denmark as BEDSTEMOR ANDS JULE-GAVE by Gutenbergus Gruppen, Copenhagen, in 1984.   ISBN: 0-394-87363-7
Manufactured in the United States of America   5 6 7 8 9 0   A B C D E F G H I J K

It was almost Christmas.

Donald Duck's nephews, Huey, Dewey, and Louie, had bought a special present for Grandma Duck.

The three boys pulled the big box through the streets to their house.

Donald found his nephews busy at work.
"What are you up to?" asked Donald.
"We're putting together a rocking chair
for Grandma's present," said Huey.
"There are lots of steps to follow,"
said Dewey.

"There are also
lots of pieces,"
said Huey.

"We have to glue
them together,"
Dewey said.

"Careful!"
Louie said
to Huey.

Finally the rocker was put together.
"Now comes the most fun—painting it!"
said Dewey.
"These flower stencils
will make it prettier,"
said Louie.

Then the boys called for Uncle Donald.
"We finished!" Huey, Dewey, and Louie said.

"A fine job you did too," said Donald.
"And just in time. Tomorrow you are going
by train to Grandma's house. You can take
the rocking chair with you then."

Early the next day Donald carried in
a big box from the garage.

The boys helped him pack the rocker
in the box.

Next they carefully tied up the box.

"Watch your paws!" Donald said to the cat.

Then everyone was ready to leave.

"Let's not forget this tag!" said Donald.

On the tag it said:

TO GRANDMA DUCK

FROM HUEY, DEWEY, AND LOUIE.

Donald and the boys took the big box
to the train station.

It had begun to snow.

Donald and Daisy and Uncle Scrooge
were going to go to Grandma's house
by sleigh.

Donald helped the conductor load
the big box in the train's baggage car.
"Good-bye! See you at Grandma's!"
Donald called to his nephews.

The train chugged along.
The boys were enjoying
the ride.

Suddenly the train stopped
with a BUMP!
The boys peered out the window.
"It's a snow slide! The train
is stuck!" said Dewey.

The snow was blocking the tracks
in front of the train.

The engineer could not drive the train
across the pile of snow and ice.

"I'm afraid we will be here for a while,"
the conductor said to the passengers.

Everyone got off the train.
The cold, fresh air felt good.

"What are we going to do?" asked Louie.
"Grandma will be worried," said Huey.
"I have an idea!" said Dewey.

Meanwhile, Grandma Duck
was waiting at her station.
"Where can those boys be?"
she wondered. "Their train
should have been here by now!"

"Do you know why the train is late?"
Grandma Duck asked the station master.
    "I heard it is stuck in the snow,"
the man said. "It will take a long time
to clear the tracks. You should go home
and wait."

Grandma walked home through the snow.
"I hope those poor boys get here
efore Christmas is over!" she said.

Meanwhile, Donald, Daisy, and Scrooge
were riding to Grandma's house
in their horse-drawn sleigh.

"What a good idea this was!" said Daisy.

"I bet the boys are at Grandma's house by now," said Donald.

"Look!" said Uncle Scrooge. "Isn't that Grandma walking up ahead of us?"

The sleigh's horses soon
caught up with the person.

It WAS Grandma!

"What are you doing here?" asked Donald.
"I thought you were home with the boys!"

Grandma Duck
told them what
had happened
to the train.

"I'm on my way
home to wait,"
Grandma said.

"We'll give you a lift," Scrooge said.
He helped Grandma into the sleigh.
"I hope the train will not be stuck
in the snow for long," said Grandma.

"We'll have to rescue the boys
somehow," Donald said to Daisy.
He did not know about Dewey's idea!

First the passengers took their skis
and packages off the train.

Then the boys tied the skis together
to make two big sleds.

Soon everyone was sledding
downhill toward town.

"Hang on tight!"
cried Dewey.

The sleds slid down the hill.
Faster and faster they went!

"Look!" shouted Grandma.
"It's the boys!"
Scrooge stopped the sleigh.

The boys tied the sleds
to the sleigh.
Then Scrooge drove
everyone to the station
in town.

The passengers were happy
to reach town before Christmas
after all!

The sleds were taken
apart.
The three boys squeezed
into Scrooge's sleigh.

Donald and Scrooge helped the boys carry
Grandma's present into her house.

"What can that be?" Grandma wondered.

"Time for bed, boys," Donald said.
"You have had a long and busy day!"

Huey, Dewey, and Louie fell asleep
in no time at all!

"Ssh," Grandma said. "They need
their sleep. There are lots of chores
for them to do tomorrow."

The boys rose early the next day.
First they shoveled snow.
Then they collected sheaves of wheat.

They hung up
the wheat for
the birds to eat.

They sawed firewood
for Grandma's stove.

Grandma was busy making pies.
The boys finished their
outdoor chores.
Then they helped
Grandma bake cookies.

There was time to play games
before dinner.

Louie said, "It's so much fun
to play—"

"Bingo!" shouted Scrooge.

Everybody helped to decorate
the Christmas tree.
Donald put the star on the top.

Then Huey, Dewey, and Louie set
the table.
Uncle Scrooge carried the plates.

Grandma Duck and Daisy
served the dinner.
What a feast they had!

The presents were under the tree.
Soon it would be time to open them.

After dinner Grandma opened up
the big present from the boys.

"Oh, my!" Grandma said happily.

"Do you like it?" asked Huey, Dewey,
and Louie.

"It's just what I needed!" Grandma said.

"The boys put that rocker together
all by themselves," Donald said.

Then the other gifts
were opened.
Daisy passed around
cups of hot cocoa.

Grandma rocked back and forth
in her new rocking chair.
"This is the best Christmas
ever!" she said. "It's wonderful
to have you all here."

It was late and time for bed.
The family looked out the window.
The sky was full of stars.

"Merry Christmas, special helpers!"
Grandma said to the boys. "You helped
the people on the train. You helped feed
the birds. You helped me with the chores.
You three helpers have given all of us
the happiest Christmas yet!"